Zealous Zeporah

Book #26 of the Spirit of Truth Storybook Series

By Linda Mason

Zealous Zeporah
Book #26 of the Spirit of Truth
Storybook Series

Author: Linda C. Mason

Published by:
Books By L. Mason
P. O. Box 1162
Powhatan, VA 23139

www.BooksbyLMason.com

Color Print:
ISBN-13: 978-1-5356-1617-1
ISBN-10: 1-5356-1617-2

Printed in the United States of America.

Zealous Zeporah

Its five O'clock in the morning and Mother won't allow me to jog that early alone, so Daddy always jog with me before school. As I got up to dress for the invigorating run this morning, I peeped out the window and noticed it was still dark outside. I usually take my shower when I get back from jogging so I would be fresh for school, so I just washed my face and brushed my teeth for now.

The sun is usually peeking over the hills of the Shenandoah Valley by the time I crossed the bridge just beyond the Madison's Middle School in my community but right now it is still dark.

It's so beautiful this time of morning and this time of year. It is early spring now and the air seems to tickle your nose when there's a slight breeze in the early morning air and just before sunset too. The smell of fresh blossoms from Dogwood trees and newly budding Tulips, has taken flight on the morning winds. The aroma of Sunflowers, Daffodils and even Butter Cups are all over the meadow. Honey bees, butterflies and ladybugs are darting from flower to flower getting their fill of whatever goodies they find in the foliage. I open my window and take a deep breath in. What a glorious morning this will be.

A variety of birds zoom by my window headed to the bird feeder Daddy mounted just for times like this. Beautiful Red birds, Blue birds, Yellow birds and Humming birds, so rich in color that they reminds me of the rich colors in a bag of Starburst candies. I sit there and take it all in just for a moment before I get dressed.

Suddenly, I was startled by a knock at my bedroom door.

"Honey, you up?" It was Daddy.

"I sure am." I answered as I pulled myself back into the reality of what I was supposed to be doing this morning.

"Give me 3 minutes, Daddy. I'll meet you on the back porch for our early morning stretch," I continued. I ran to the bathroom, washed my face and brushed my teeth. I had picked out my jogging outfit before I went to bed and it was already hanging in the bathroom. So I finished dressing, ran down stairs to pick up my bottle of water and met Daddy on the back porch as planned.

After stretching, we found our regular jogging trail and enthusiastically headed out for our 5 mile round trip. We talked about the track team at school and about the fact that I had been selected *Team Captain* this year by my classmates. Everyone thought I had some good ideas for staying in excellent shape. After all, I was extremely zealous and demonstrated characteristics of a great role model for the rest of the team. I was very discipline with physical activities like after school track practices. Additionally, I was consistently jogging on my own outside of school activities. On Saturdays, I encouraged my teammates to meet at my house and jog the same trail that Daddy and I was on this morning. I seemed to be the most enthusiastic person on the track team.

Daddy and I always have so much fun jogging, joking, singing and planning events during our early morning jogs. I get to hear about some of the most hilarious things he did as a child growing up and he seems so interested in listening about the things that are important to me. I feel like I am in paradise when I jog in the mornings before school. Life can't get any better than this.

"Oops!" I said as I felt myself falling to the ground.

"Ouch!" I cried out feeling my ankle twist on the way down. Dad reached out to try and break my fall but he couldn't. I hit the ground fast and hard.

Daddy knelt down immediately beside me on the ground.

"Zippy, Are you Okay?" Daddy asked. He called me Zippy when he was either excited about something I did or if he had something very serious to share with me. I could tell right away that this fall was serious.

"Oh, Daddy! My ankle! It hurts so badly!" I cried out as I grabbed my ankle where the pain had started to throb immediately.

As Daddy took a closer look at my ankle, he noticed that swelling had already begun.

"Hang on, Zippy. I'll need to lift you and carry you back home so that we can put ice on it and get you to the hospital," he said with a very concerned expression on his face. Even through that serious look, he looked at me with a smile and said,

"I know it hurts now, Zippy but it will heal and it will heal very soon."

"But Daddy, I have a track met in a week?" I replied with tears running down my face.

"And you will be there, Zippy. You will be there," he said with the most sincere tone in his voice I have ever heard. I looked up at him, carrying me back down the trail as though I was as light as a cotton cloud. So I agreed.

"Yes, you are right. I will be there. I will never let my team down!"

"That's my girl," Daddy said as he kissed me on the cheek.

The ride to the hospital seemed to take forever but I was already planning strategies for my team to win without depending on me as a runner.

Daddy rode in the back with me and I asked the medical team on board if they had a pen and paper. They allowed me to elevate my head a little on the stretcher but I had my leg elevate now because of the swelling. My ankle was surrounded with a fancy ice pack and they took it on and off every few minutes or so.

I asked them to give the pen and pad to my daddy and I also asked Dad to take some notes for me. My ankle had stopped throbbing so badly but my mind was racing so fast I didn't know if I could tell my dad everything I was thinking.

"Daddy?" I called out as soon as they put the pen and pad in his hands.

"Would you take down a few notes for me? This is the new line up for the Relay Race at the Track Meet next week. Rodger is taking the first quarter followed by Tonya. Then Cynthia is running third and Cortez will bring it home for us. I'm still Team Captain and we are going to win! It's not about one person anyway. It's about the team!" I said in almost a *cheer-like* tone of voice.

I felt excitement rising up in me, even though the unknown outcome of this injury. Daddy wrote down what I had asked him to, tucked the note in his pocket and soon we were pulling up at the hospital.

The ambulance attendants wheeled me through the doors of the emergency entrance on the gurney but then transferred me to a wheel chair.

Daddy got me registered and then came the long wait in the waiting room until my name was called.

The waiting room was packed with all kinds of injured people, including some children that were crying. I looked around at the parents of one crying child trying to comfort him but with very little success. I looked up at Daddy with pleading eyes and he looked back at me and said,

"Go ahead, Zippy." He knew I wouldn't be able to sit there watching all of these sad children and not get involved. I rolled my wheelchair over to a little boy that was crying. He seemed to be around five years old. I looked up at his parents and asked if I could talk to him. They said I could so I looked at him and said,

"Hi. My name is Zeporah. What's your name?" Through tears he said,

"Shaun. My name is Shaun." I showed him my foot wrapped in an ice bag and said to him,

"Shaun, I'm a track star. I was jogging with my dad this morning when I fell and hurt my ankle. I think it's broken and I'm sure I will get a very pretty cast put on it in a little while. Do you want to be the first one to sign my cast?"

The little boy stopped crying immediately and smiled at me as he replied,

"Really? But what does *sign my cast* mean?" Even though he seemed a little confused about the whole thing, at least he had stopped crying.

"Well Shaun, they will probably put a giant bandage on my ankle so that it won't move while it heals. The bandage will sometimes come in pretty colors and people like to draw pretty designs on it or sometimes even write their names on it. They call that hard bandage a cast," I explain.

"It's usually pretty cool."

"Do you know how to write your name Shaun?" I then asked.

"I sure do. Don't I, Momma?" Shaun answered.

"I have been practicing my name for a long, long time and I'm working on writing my last name now. My last name is Winston. Sometimes I forget to put the 't' after the 's' but I do pretty good most of the times. Can I put my first and my last name on your cast, Miss Zip?" He asked with the biggest smile on his face.

"You surely can, Shaun. Well, yes you can if your parents think that it's okay, but you have to promise me one thing first." I responded.

"What's that?" Shaun asked. "What do I have to promise you?"

"Well, Shaun. You have to promise me that you will be very brave getting your treatment. Can you promise me that? I know it hurts and you may need to cry a little but then you've got to dry those eyes and be a big boy."

"Oh, I can be v**e**ry brave. I really can!" He said with a smile and then he imitated a movement usually made by the Incredible Hulk. However, when he tried to flex his arms, he screame**d** out in pain -- "Ouch!

Oh, I forgo**t** I cut my arm when I fell against a tree branch this morning. But I can be brave. I really can!" He said again after he very gently patted his bandaged arm. He then lo**o**ked up at his parents and asked,

"Mommy, Dadd**y.** Can we wait until Miss Zee is finished so that I can be the first one to sign her cast?"

I guess he couldn't remember **o**r couldn't pronounce my whole name so he called me Miss Zee. That was okay with me. They said of course he could sign my cast and told me thanks. The hospital attendants then called his name and as they took him back into the treatment area, he turned to me and said,

"I'll be waiting for you." I told him alright and then Shaun, along with his parents, disappeared through the door.

"That was a very sweet thing you did for the little boy, Zeporah," Daddy said to me.

"Oh, I'm glad I could help, Daddy." I said as another attendant came through the doors they had taken Shaun through and called two other people before finally calling my name.

Within the next two hours, both Shaun and I had finished up our treatment and were released from the hospital. Shaun's parents had allowed him to wait for me. With his arm bandaged up and my leg in a cast, from my toes to under my knee, Shaun had placed his name with his signature smiley face on my cast.

Now it was time to concentrate on the track team. When I got home, now sporting a set of cool crutches that had diagonal stripes on them, I sat down in the living room by the computer and began to send pictures of my new cast on Face Book along with other information about our new winning strategy and practice schedule to my team mates. There was no time to sit around feeling sorry for myself. I had a lot of planning to do regardless of my ankle. After all, I'm still the team captain. We also needed more practices considering the new line up before our competition on Saturday. Dad had called my coach already from the hospital so he had the heads up on all of my suggestions for the new strategic relay team.

We were planning a practice relay this afternoon at 6pm. Right now I was on pain medication so I felt no pain; however, I was very sleepy. After Daddy fixed me a sandwich for a quick lunch, we all decided, including Mom, that it would be a good idea for me to take a short nap before we met at the school's track. Dad knew me very well and knew I wasn't about to sit this one out. Momma was in agreement with all of this too. I was known as Zealous Zeporah and a broken ankle wasn't about to slow me down ... Well, maybe just a little. So I stretched out on the sofa and took a nap.

When I woke up, I could feel a little throbbing going on throughout my entire leg but taking another pain pill would put me to sleep again, so I decided to deal with the aching until after we met at the track. Mom asked me if I was alright and I told her that I could hang, so I got a bottle of water and we loaded up and drove to the track.

With the new line-up for the relay, we only needed to go through it twice and I'd be headed back home to put my leg up. As we pulled up to the school, I looked across the field and saw everyone there stretching.

"Great!" I thought. They are doing exactly what I taught them to do. I was so proud of this track team because they were extremely focused, just like me. Well, almost everyone. Rodger was our team comedian. He had some strong legs on him but he chose to play around a lot and tell jokes all the time.

Originally, I was supposed to take the first leg of the relay because of my speed. We had planned on me getting a significant lead before I passed the baton to my next team mate. I chose Rodger to replace me for this race. Rodger and I have been very consistent in finishing the 100 meter in 10 seconds and sometimes less. Tonya is hitting 12 to 13 seconds consistently and Cynthia is about the same, so their placement in the relay will not change. Cortez has excellent speed also. Additionally, he is very good at sprinting to make up ground if necessary.

We are scheduled to do a Four by One hundred meter relay, which means that each participant (four runners) will run 100 yards each before passing the baton to the next person in line, totaling 400 meters in all. Our regular practice schedule is once a week. Of course, my normal practice on my own was at least four out of seven days a week even when there were no races planned. However, there is a race scheduled for this coming Saturday so we needed to practice every day until then. Half of our practice time this week will be geared towards passing the baton. Our *hand-offs* had to be solid. We also must make sure that we all make the exchange properly without running out of the *exchange zone, which would cause us to be disqualified.*

We had purchased new batons for this year made of anodized lightweight metal with rounded safety ends instead of the plastic ones we had been using before. I guess both kinds are fine but the new metal ones surely made us feel like we were running with the pros.

When everyone arrived this evening, Coach Tyler was the first to meet me at the car and helped me out. The cast was all the way up my leg to my knee and the doctor said that it will probably take six to eight weeks before it comes off. I was feeling pretty good except for a slight throbbing so using my crutches, I made my way over to the field where all of my team mates wanted to sign my cast. I told them that there would be plenty of time for all of that later; but for now, we needed to get our practice in. Coach Tyler agreed and we started to discuss our new strategy followed with more warm-up stretches. It was established that today would be all about gripping that baton properly and passing it in a timely manner within the designated exchange zone. Practice went very well that evening and the next, except for all of Rodger's constant jokes. I didn't miss a beat with helping in the area of motivating my team; however, it took additional concentration to not allow Rodger to get under my skin with his jokes. Nevertheless, his running was on target so I just pushed on.

Our last two days of practice would be spent stepping up our speed. We wanted to push for a time of 10 seconds each 100 yard sprint. It shouldn't take but one or two seconds to pass off the baton. A great finish would be completed in 40 to 45 seconds. Right now without me, we were averaging 50 seconds. That may not be enough to pull off a win. We were competing against one of the best track teams in the state. Mt. Vernon Middle was the best in our division. We had anticipated breaking their record with a win of our own this year because of the speed I had been able to achieve coupled with Cortez's incredible speed and stamina. Cynthia and Tonya were really good too, averaging 13 seconds each for a one hundred meter run. Even though things have been altered due to my mishap; as team captain, I won't allow this team to lose any ground. Regardless of all that has happened, I was determined that we will win this year!

The next two days went very well knocking off two to four seconds on our time. I seemed to be managing pretty well with my new limitations even though sometimes it was irritating and I missed the morning jogs with my dad. We all got through it all somehow and the day of the big event had finally arrived.

At breakfast that morning, I didn't have an appetite at all so I just sipped a little orange juice and grabbed a banana to take with me to the track. I was ready to get this thing done. Mom and Dad were finishing up their morning routines and cleaned up. So I sat on the front porch swing and tried to calm myself down. I was so excited in anticipation of all that was about to take place, that I had forgotten to put on my team Jersey. I hobbled back into the house to get it. It was upstairs in my room, so it took me a little while to get it and head back down stairs. By the time I did, Mom and Dad were ready to roll.

The morning was breezy, but sunny -- perfect for this special event. Mom had packed a cooler full of water and some fresh fruit for snacks and energy pick-me-ups. As we headed to the track today, visions of a perfect win was all I could see. We had planned to get to the track early so that all of my team mates could finally sign my cast. I hadn't allowed time for that during our earlier practices. I had brought along a box of multi-colored, permanent makers and we planned to have a great time before warm-ups autographing my cast, which up until now, only had Shaun's name on it with a smiley face he had drawn.

When we pulled up, everyone ran to meet us at the car. As Dad opened the back car door for me, I swung my legs around to hang out of the car door and handed everyone the box of markers. I sat there with my legs hanging off the side of the car seat watching this nutty group stormed the door as if I was some big celebrity or something. I didn't mind this time, though. I knew it was just their way of letting off some steam to relax everyone before the race, so we enjoyed every moment.

Rodger had lots of usual jokes as he drew a cheetah on my cast beside his name to represent how strong and fast he was. When they all had finished, I did notice that I was a bit hungry now so Mom handed me the banana I had brought along. After some light joking, we all headed to the track for warm-ups. Other teams had started to arrive and the area began to buzz with the sound of a very excited crowd all supporting their favorite teams. The smell of grilled hot dogs, hamburger, with onions and green peppers had begun to fill the air already. I even thought I could smell some fresh popcorn among the many aromas floating by. It was going to be a triumphant day indeed.

The moment of truth was finally here. Everyone took their places around the track. There were four teams in all and ours were positioned in the second lane. Rodger looked my way one last time before he took his position with the baton tightly gripped in his hand. All other participants took their places around the track at the 100 meter marks. My heart was pounding so hard, that I thought I would end up back in the emergency room this time for some kind of heart malfunction. All of a sudden, I heard someone calling me.

"Miss Zip! Miss Zip! Miss Zip!" I heard coming from somewhere on the field to my right. I looked up and saw that it was Shaun and his parents. Shaun was in a sprint, running towards me and his parents were following; doing a terrible job trying to keep up with him. As he reached me, he hugged me so hard that I thought I would fall over.

"Shaun!" I called out to him once I could pry him off of my good leg.

"What are you doing here? How did you know I would be here today?" I asked.

"Mom and Dad kept up with the news on TV and you told me that you were a star runner. I knew you would be here. I just knew it. So I talked Mom into coming today. I've been looking for you all morning and now I found you," Shaun explained, now out of breath from talking so fast.

Then we heard the horn buzz for the race to begin. I turned from Shaun and gazed at the track field. Things were so tense in the air, I knew my heart skipped a beat. Shouts and screams from all around me with people rooting for their own teams came blaring forth but I couldn't make a sound. Soon I was in my own world and the screeching sounds all around me seemed to just stop. All I could focus on was our relay team doing what we had practiced to do. My eyes went from each person on my team, first Rodger and then Cynthia. Next came Tonya and finally, Cortez.

It was time to pass the baton in seconds and as the second runner began to jog with their hand extended behind them for the pass-off, the neck-n-neck team member to the left of them, slipped and fell on the field. I grabbed my stomach hoping that they wouldn't fall across our lane and knock Rodger over. I could hear the entire crowd scream out

"Ahhhhhhh!" including myself, at the same split second.

Now snatched back to reality, I couldn't believe what had just happened. The runner got back up without falling into anyone else's lane but was now seconds behind the other runners. Everyone proceeded around the rest of the track and after two more baton pass-offs, Cortez was sprinting to the finish line. The people in the stands were electric! Cortez and a person named Toni, where neck-to-neck nearing the finish line.

"Go Cortez! Go!" I screamed as I beat my crutches up against the fence I was standing next to.

"Go Cortez! Go!" Shaun screamed imitating me, as he hit his little fist against the fence.

We didn't win that day but we did come in two seconds behind the winning team. We ran the fastest one by four hundred relay we had ever run and I was so proud of my team. I don't think we could have done any better if I had been able to run with them. We celebrated our team's personal victory way into the evening at my home.

Now finally getting a little rest sitting back on my porch swing, I looked down at my broken ankle and say, "I'm in paradise. Life can't get any better than this."

Spirit of Truth Storybook
Activity Page

1. *After reading the story, ask yourself the following questions:*

- What did you like about the story?

- What would you change about the story?

- What could you have done to make things turn out differently?

- Can you think of a way to help others after reading this story?

2. *Go back through the story pages and **decode** your **secret message**.*

- Write the message on the lines below.

- Send it to me through email at: www.BooksbyLMason.com

I will send you back a personal comment. Be sure to include your gender and age.

Dove Letter Cutout

Receive *15% discount coupon* off of the purchase of my Editor's Edition of "**The Spirit of Truth**" Storybook Series, with proof of purchase from A - Z. This special edition will contain all 26 stories within one volume along with some added goodies. Fill out the chart below and **please** **print** all information clearly.

A	B	C	D	E	F
G	H	I	J	K	L
M	N	O	P	Q	R
S	T	U	V	W	X
Y	Z				

Glue your *"**Dove Letter**"* cutouts in the corresponding boxes, on top of the proper letter. Fill 26 spaces from A- Z. Then cut this page out and mail it to:

**Linda Mason
P. O box 1162
Powhatan, VA 23139**

Name ____

Address ____**State** ________

Zip ____________ **Email** ____

Wacky Facts
I'll Bet you Didn't Know

- It is impossible to lick your own elbow. (try it)

- A crocodile cannot stick its tongue out.

- A shrimp's heart is in its head.

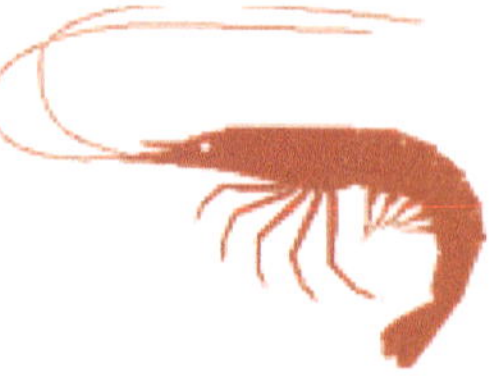

- It is physically impossible for pigs to look up into the sky.

- ·The "sixth sick sheik's sixth sheep's sick" is believed to be the toughest tongue twister in the English language.

- Like fingerprints, everyone's tongue print is different.

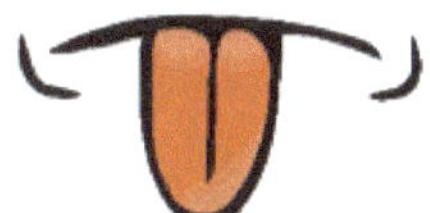

- There are 293 ways to make change for a dollar

- A cat has 32 muscles in each ear.

More Wacky Facts

- Tigers have striped skin, not just striped fur.

- An Ostrich's eye is bigger than its brain.

- Rubber bands last longer when refrigerated.

- Some lipsticks contain fish scales.

- Cat urine glows under a black-light.

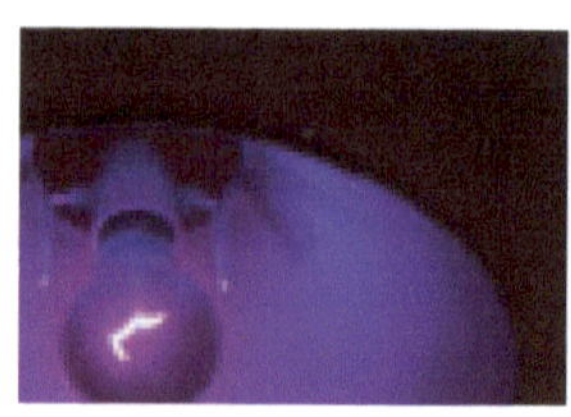

Now that you know, let's take a quiz

1. It is impossible to lick your own ___

    a. Foot

    b. Knee

    c. Elbow

2. A shrimp's heart is in its ___

    a. Stomach

    b. Eyes

    c. Head

3. A cat has 32 muscles in each ___

    a. Ear

    b. Toe

    c. Hand

4. Rubber bands last longer when ___

    a. Frozen

    b. Washed

    c. Refridgerated

S.O.T. Message of Encouragement Worksheet

(Fill in the missing letters on a <u>separate sheet of paper</u> or here, if you own the storybook, to unlock your secret message)

Zealous Zeporah

E _ _ h _ s _ _ s _   _ _ _ _   _ _ n _ _ r _ _ _

_ _ _   g _   _   _ _ _ g   _ _ y _

_ _ _ _ _   _ t   _ _ m _ _   _ _   l _ _ e' _

_ s _ _ _ _ _ .   _ t _ _   c _ _ _ _ t _ _ _

_ _   y _ _ _   _ r _ _ _ _   a _ _   _ _

_ f _ _ _   _ h _ _   w _ _ _

e _ _ _ _ _ s _ _ _ m   _ _ _   s _ _ c _ _ _ _ _ _ .

** The meaning of the word "<u>Enthusiasm</u>" is to be very sure, passionate, and excited about something. Your heart feels warm and fuzzy every time you think about it.*

Spirit of Truth Storybook Series

APPROPRIATE AGE LEVEL

COLOR CODING KEY

The reading level for these stories is grade 5, but they can be understood and enjoyed by younger children, when read to them by older children or adults. The storybook covers have been colored to reflect the average comprehension levels for the following age groups.

Ages 4 and 5 = GREEN

Ages 6 and 7 = BLUE

Ages 8 and 9 = ORANGE

Ages 10 and above = RED

A special inspirational message has been coded throughout each story to help create 'added focus,' as well as, a visual tool for interactive concentration. ___Decode your secret message (written in red lettering throughout the story)___ *and send it to me, along with your name and age, through my personal email address on my website at ___www.BooksByLMason.com___ and you will receive a personal email response from me. Some of the letters of the secret message have already been provided to assist you in your decoding. Additionally, an added bonus finger puppet activity, brain games,* *puzzles or other goodies, awaits each reader in the back of every storybook. An added "Treasure Hunt" can be found throughout the illustrations from my collection of storybooks, which **details of this treasure hunt can only be found on my website.**

Also, E-Book Editions of this collection of storybooks, having no activities in the back of the books, as well as A Collector's Edition of this 26 Storybook Series is forthcoming. The collector's edition will include all 26 stories in the same book or 2 Volumes; at which time, the Master's List of every inspirational message will be revealed.*

1. ***Anxious Arlene:*** This story is about an *anxious* family consisting of a young brother and sister who lives with their grandpa and grandma. They have a little adopted dog that was never claimed or found by the original owner, and they all live together (with a few mishaps), in a loving, exciting home. This story can be enjoyed by children ages five and up.

2. ***Busy Benny:*** This story is about a busy little boy who loves to tinker with Wacky car models. He gets the opportunity to create a child sized Wacky car, with the help of his mom and dad, and finally enters it into a race with him doing the driving. He runs into a little surprise during his test run. This story can be enjoyed by children ages seven and up.

3. ***Catty Carla:*** This story is about a group of neighborhood house cats who carry on 'catty' conversations behind their friend's back at times. One particular Burmese cat soon realizes that her behavior was not appropriate, and it could be a little late for apologies. This story deals with death portrayed through animal characters. This book is dedicated to my daughter, Tamara, who as an adult, loss a cat she adored, Jeckle, to an illness. The story line is very light; however, use parental wisdom. This story can be enjoyed by children ages five and up.

4. ***Doubtful Denise:*** This story is about a single father raising a young teenaged daughter who is full of doubt about herself, her abilities, and her future. Through a father's persistent encouragement and unyielding love for her, she eventually gains trust in herself and finds hope for a brighter future. This story can be enjoyed by children ages seven and up.

5. *Excited Ernesto:* This story is about a teenaged boy overcoming a fear of riding roller coasters. He experiences some exciting events at the county fair with a buddy friend of his and his buddy's sister, Maria. She adds extra excitement for Ernesto because no one knew she would be there, and he has a secret crush on her. Join this exciting group of youth as they sample the tasty treats found at all State Fairs, and as they experience some of the thrills of riding a roller coaster for the first time. Ride along with Ernesto, as your heart races to the beat of his own. This story can be enjoyed by children ages seven and up.

6. *Fearless Freddie:* Freddie is a little boy who is very creative and willing to test out any new adventure, regardless of risk. He is always ready and willing to try dangerous stunts until one day it gets him into big trouble. Does he learn from making dangerous choices, or does he continue to believe he is *invincible?* This story can be enjoyed by children ages five and up.

7. *Graceful Gregory:* Gregory loves to dance. He encounters teasing by his peers, but continues to do what he loves. He eventually meets another little boy who is not so interested in dancing, but his family is insisting that he gives it a try. The two boys meet and things begin to change for both of them. This story can be enjoyed by children ages seven and up, but younger if the reader is already dancing.

8. *Hopeful Henry:* Henry is full of anticipation for the new school year and is hopeful he will not experience the disappointments he has had in the past. He apparently gets disappointed over, and over again until a tragedy occurs in his life and he ends up being supported by the very people he thought were insignificant. He learns also, not only to see things differently, but to always be grateful and remain hopeful. This story can be enjoyed by children ages seven and up.

9. *Itchy Irvin:* This story is played out using a pack of dogs as characters. One of them misjudges some physical symptoms of another dog, and begins teasing him. That dog gets picked on constantly because of a skin condition. This particular *pack of dogs* meets a little boy who is going through a similar situation with his classmates at school. Let's see how this doggy story barks out. This story can be enjoyed by children ages seven and up.

10. *Jumping Josey:* This story is about a teenager who lives a life of thrills, while flipping and jumping, every chance she gets. She ultimately gets to experience one of her life's dreams -- sky diving. Travel with Josey as she goes on the most exhilarating jump of her life. This story can be enjoyed by children ages seven and up.

11. *Kissing Kirkland:* This story is about a very affectionate little boy who spends his days and nights kissing all kinds of creatures. Eventually, his normal kissing routine lands him into big trouble when he gets attacked by a momma duck. Let's follow our adorable *Kissing Kirkland* through an average day at home and see how he survives some of the repercussions having a personality like this, may present. This story can be enjoyed by children ages five and up.

12. *Lonely Lucilia:* This story is about two teenagers that are best friends. They are forced to separate, due to a family relocation, to a different country. The storyline starts out in a coastal town in Fife, Scotland, where Lucilia and Dillard have lived all of their lives. Take this lonesome journey with Lucilia, as she is forced to move from the only place she's ever known, and from her very best friend in the world, to a strange country she knows nothing about -- the United States of America. This story can be enjoyed by children ages eight and up.

13. *Muddy Maria:* This story explores the life of a little girl who loves to get dirty. With the help of her creative mother, her *dirty,* playful habit is channeled into a very productive fun activity. Dive in to this interesting twist of events and discover how playing in a lot of dirt, in some situations, can possibly turn out to be good for you. This story can be enjoyed by children ages five and up.

14. *Noisy Nelly:* This story explores the hatching of a bird from a bird's perspective. As this special bird explores her new world, words of wisdom flow from its mother. These words eventually take root in Nelly's heart in a very unique way. Soar with Nelly as she learns a very important lesson by refocusing her perspective on a part of her life she once perceived as gloomy. This story is dedicated to my first grandchild, Niyah Nylliana Mason, whom I believe one day will also soar as high as an eagle. This story can be enjoyed by children ages seven and up.*Orphaned Ophelia:* Most of this story takes place in a very unique orphanage.

Ophelia lives with the discomforts of not having a traditional family, but through it all she finds the compassion to help others. One day that compassion is returned, and she receives the most rewarding surprise of her life. This story can be enjoyed by children ages five and up.

15. *Pudgy Pete:* This story is about a little boy who obviously, because of his nickname, carries a little more weight than the average child. Journey with Pete as his self-pity and low self-esteem evolves into self-worth. After befriending a new *physically challenged* neighbor who moves in next door, she teaches him how to appreciate the special person he is, and not to focus on what size pants he wears. This story can be enjoyed by children ages seven and up.

16. *Quarrelsome Quaniqua:* This story contains **sensitive** material. It is not intended to be read as a *bedtime* story. Our story deals with a serious issue that some children must live with every day: ***an abusive living environment*** (non-sexual)*.* The main character is a Latino teen (Quaniqua) who lives in poor, none-nurturing conditions. She becomes bitter and her behavior follows suit, until she meets someone outside of the home, and of a different culture, who finally treats her with respect. This causes Quaniqua to pull herself up and out of the pit she seemed to be falling into. Hang in there with her through the hard times, and see this young lady become a more productive, happier citizen. This story can be enjoyed by children eight and up; however, use parental wisdom as to if this story is suited for your particular younger child.

17. *Reckless Ricardo:* This story is about a young boy who starts out with some very reckless and disrespectful behaviors, but ends up with a very unusual science project that helps him start behaving in new, more respectful ways. You might be surprised at the results of this nontraditional outcome to a very common allergy. This story can be enjoyed by children ages seven and up.

18. *Shy Stanley:*   This story is about a very quiet little boy who has some very interesting talents. He spends a lot of his time alone; however, he is extremely observant. Stanley meets a little girl with similar gifts and interests, which creates a bond

that opens them both up to view their world differently. Let's visit these interesting young people and discover what their talents are. Maybe you have similar talents as well, and might have some interesting ideas of your own as to how to present those talents to the world. This story can be enjoyed by children ages seven and up.

19. *Tearful Tanya*: This story deals with a little girl who is full of grief over the passing of her grandmother. The family has a spiritual upbringing, and the little girl's mom guides her through the grieving process as she draws strength from above, where she's convinced her grandmother now resides. This story may be a little sensitive if you are a child in a similar situation, yet it can be enjoyed by children ages five and above.

20. *Ungrateful Ursula*: This story contains '**sensitive**' material. It is recommended for children ages ten and above. The story deals with a teenaged girl who grew up without her mother, and who very rarely saw her father. She lives temporarily with her aging grandmother. However, because of her grandmother's illness, Ursula must now live with her father, and she begins to use '*cutting*' as her method of coping. Things smooth out, but it's a very bumpy, painful ride. Walk with Ursula as she moves from '*much pain*' to '*much gain.*' This story can be enjoyed and read by children ages ten and above.

21. *Valiant Vivica*: This story is about a very gifted little girl who loves contact sports. Boys her same age seem to both admire her, and can be intimidated by her unprecedented strength at the same time. A natural disaster occurs on the day of Vivica's first wrestling tournament, and her valiant personality takes over. Follow along as she demonstrates extraordinary acts of bravery, and through it all, this experience will change her forever. This story can be enjoyed by children ages eight and above.

22. *Worrying Winston*: This story is about a little boy whose mother is an active Marine in the United States' Armed Forces. Winston is a very responsible little boy; however, he does worry a great deal about his mother's well-being. While on a *Treasure Hunt*, a game designed by his mother using riddles written in a letter Winston received, an unfortunate accident

occurs and his mother ends up with a serious injury. Will they complete the Treasure Hunt? Stand with Winston and his father as they draw strength from each other to deal with a life's situation that changes their entire world. This story can be enjoyed by children ages eight and above.

23. *X-Con Xavier*: This story has been presented in *'limerick style poetry'* to lighten the seriousness of the topic for a child. Because of Xavier's destructive behavior, he is placed in various state institutions. Xavier meets a person while incarcerated that offers him hope and a different way of thinking. His inner spiritual change eventually points him in a new direction. Now with new hope, he has a chance to begin a new, more productive lifestyle outside of lock-up. This story can be enjoyed and read by children ages ten and above.

24. *Yearning Yolanda*: This story takes you on a short journey with a twelve year old young girl who lost her eyesight in a car accident a year ago. She yearns for life to be as it was before the accident; however, life has a way of throwing you constant challenges that could cause you to either withdraw further into bitterness, or to emerge with a heart of gratefulness. Which one will Yolanda choose? Walk with Yolanda through an even harder challenge that, if handled with fear and bitterness, could not only take her life, but the lives of her mother and her best friend, Toby (her dog). This story can be enjoyed by children ages eight and above.

25. *Zealous Zeporah*: Zeporah is a very passionate young lady full of enthusiasm for life. She jogged regularly, but one day she slipped and fell injuring her ankle. A situation such as this would have brought most people to a halt, or perhaps could cause others to go into a state of temporary depression. How will Zeporah handle a situation like this, when so many people are depending on her enthusiasm to help motivate them? This story can be enjoyed by children ages seven and above.

About The Author

Minister Linda Mason is a unique ministry gift to the Body of Christ. Her experiences include the establishment of *Spirit of Praise Liturgical Outreach, Inc.*, a non-profit 501 © 3 organization, which not only helped to establish and oversee new dance ministries, but also extended into the communities.

In addition to the *Spirit of Truth Storybook Series*, Minister Linda has published *Appetizers from the Word of God… Are You Hungry?* Volumes 1, 2, & 3; which is an awesome tool for teaching foundational truths, in a simplistic manner, from God's Word.

Linda is a native of Suffolk, Virginia, the wife of George B. Mason, Jr., the mother of three adult children, Tamara, Tiena, and George III. She has two adorable grandchildren, Niyah and Laana. Linda holds an Associate Degree in Early Childhood Education and has a passion for writing. She has written and is in the process of publishing these 26 children's stories from A to Z. Her plan is to have these unique stories available in both English and Spanish in the near future.

What others have stated about this Series

- *Author Linda Mason's book, "Kissing Kirkland", is one of a series of books that tells a delightful story with a secret hidden valuable message for children. Her stories will captivate her audience with a variety of age appropriate activities to enhance each child's learning. As an educator for many years, I highly recommend her books!* **By Amelia Hopkins, a high school counselor.**

- *Linda Mason has done an excellent job using her creativity and insight in writing this series of books, the **Spirit of Truth Storybook Series from A-Z**. Each book deals with a subject or situation,* *such as a particular disability, or set-back that a child might encounter and have difficulty dealing with. The books offer resolutions that are positive and encouraging, helping a child build strength, confidence and maturity. The activities in the back of each book reinforce the lesson learned. The graphics are colorful and eye-catching, and each book's vocabulary is age appropriate. Each book is color coded to fit each age group, so there are appropriate books for every child's age. These are books your children will want to read or hear over and over; read by a big sister or brother. And they also have the opportunity to communicate with the author directly! I highly recommend these books for your children and grandchildren!* **By Nona J. Mason, a retired teacher, mother and grandmother.**

www.ingramcontent.com/pod-product-compliance
Lightning Source LLC
Chambersburg PA
CBHW041411010726
47507CB00001B/79